Chaos in da Chi

Latisha Miller

New Book Authors Publishing—Madison, WI
ISBN: 979-8-9861190-5-2
Library of Congress Control Number: 2022910226
Title: Chaos in da Chi
Author: Latisha Miller
Digital distribution | 2022
Paperback | 2022

Dedication

I dedicate my first book to my children. They are my reason of why I don't give up. Whatever it is in life you wanna do, go for it! I wanna thank my parents and sister Jelisa for the support. I appreciate all you guys have done for me and my two children, thank you to all my supporters. I hope you enjoy my first book there's more to come because it's always Chaos in da Chi

Chapter One

Hey, my name is Aneka Brown. I'm from the southside of Chicago. I love my city and shit, it's always something or someone to do lol.

I love to shop. I ain't got no kids, so I'm free to be me and my girl Jasmine is too, aka Jazzy. Now as for my other girl Markell, that's my bitch and all, but she keep getting pregnant by these bum ass niggas. She on baby number 4, yep.

It's Thursday it's hot as hell outside. Coming up on the weekend, so I'm definitely stepping out. I money and even tho, I don't work all the time, like I do a little CNA work from time to time.

Ima hustlers, I hustle men out of money. I stay fly like a motherfucker. From my head to my pretty ass toes. These men keep me keep me right, married or not. I don't care as long as they giving me everything I want. Fuck they bitches. I can take any bitch man. I been seeing this guy name Brian Blake.

He from the city too but he lives in the suburbs. He's a big time Lawyer. He's married with three kids. We met downtown at some fancy bar. I had on this super tight short dress, open toe shoes, I had my 18" hair extension in looking sexy as fuck. He had on a black suit with a blue scrip shirt, red bottom shoes. I knew he had money. He had a beard, hair cut low, and he was coming right my way.

I was sipping my sex on the beach and he said, "How you doing beautiful?"

I said, "I'm fine and you?"

He replied, "Oh you definitely fine what you drinking?"

I said, "Sex on the beach."

"Can I buy you another one?" he said.

"Of course." With a smile I gave. Oh my lord, this man was fine and smelled so good.

That's how we met. We talked, he told me about his wife and kids. I gave him just a few things about me because I don't get close to these niggas. But it's something about him I really like.

He asked for my number and we went on our first date to a nice little restaurant downtown. Brian is a man I'm really interested in. All the other guy's I use to play with, fuck them, take they money, and think nothing of it.

Brian is different and I'm feeling a way about him. A feeling I never felt before. He's in a marriage he wants out of. I'm single and I wanted him. It was his honesty, his confidence, his love for his kids and career, and the way he treated me.

He was respectful and I'm determined to make him mine.

＊──❊◆❊──＊

Chapter Two

"**J**asmine Jasmine."

"What?"

"Girl come down here. Got me yelling your name out here all ghetto and shit lol."

"I'm coming downstairs now bitch. What's up bitch how are things with ya?" said Jasmine.

"Cool same old shit," said Aneka. "You know I wanna go to this party, downtown you wanna go?"

"Downtown hell no," said Jasmine. "Why you like partying with them stuck up motherfuckers?"

"Girl that's where the money at foreal foreal."

"Aww you only saying that cause you met your boo Brian there."

Both laughed.

"You been acting crazy since you met him," said Jasmine.

"Why you say that?" said Aneka.

"Cause bitch you don't fuck with yo hood niggas like you use to."

"Well my baby make sure I'm good," said Aneka.

"Is that so?" said Jasmine. "So what he doing about his wife?"

"Jazzy, why you gotta go there?"

Both laughed.

"Foreal I thought you said he was leaving her ass," said Jasmine.

"He is he's just waiting for the right time," said Aneka.

"Ok if you say so," said Jasmine.

"Have you heard from Tarell?" asked Aneka.

Tarell Davis was Jasmine's boyfriend. He's tall and dark, nice body. He just came home from prison after doing 3 years for selling drug. He has 3 kids and jazzy was dying to have his baby. Why, I don't know. All he do is lie and cheat on her but she loved him.

"Yes Tarell home boo," said Jasmine. "And I can't wait to see him tonight."

"Wait, wait, wait," said Aneka. "He been home since Tuesday and you still ain't seen him?"

"Nope," said Jasmine. "You know how it is girl. He had shit to take care of, but tonight is our night."

Both laughed.

"All shit," said Aneka.

Both laughed.

"There go Markell ass," said Jasmine.

"What's up bitches," said Markell.

"Girl where you just coming from?" said Aneka.

"Shit home. What y'all hoe's finna get into?" said Markell.

"Well I'm finna see my nigga later," said Jazzy. "Aneka wanted me to go to a party downtown, but that's not my party spot."

"All well I'll go Neka," said Markell.

"Cool," said Aneka. "Be ready at 7pm bitch."

"Where was you headed tho?" asked Jasmine to Markell.

"To pick up DJ bad ass from his granny house," said Markell. "Then back home on my porch. Dame, it's hot as hell out here."

"What y'all doing for the 4th of July?" asked Markell.

"Shit me and Brian got plans," said Aneka.

"Shit I don't know," said Jasmine. "Tarell just came home."

"All yeah sure did," said Markell. "Bitch he take yo ass down yet?"

Both laughed.

"Hell naw, but tonight don't call my phone."

Both laughed.

"Ok bitch," said Markell.

Playing loud music from Jasmine appt was Tink song, Ain't got time today. Aneka couldn't help but to think of Brian.

His smell, touch, and kiss. Dame I can't wait to see him at his friend Darnell Bailey party. Darnell knew about me and Brian. And didn't like that Brian was with me because he's married. But Brian is his childhood friend so he rolled with it.

Aneka and Markell went home. Jasmine got dressed because Tarell was on his way. Tarell pulled up in a 2021 BMW X3 white truck. Jasmine jumped right in. Tarell was very attractive but also a bad guy like most women love.

Chapter Three

"Hey Stranger," said Tarell

"I missed you," said Jasmine. "What you been up to since you been home?"

"Shit business seeing my people," said Tarell.

"But what took you so long to come see me?" asked Jasmine.

"Saving the best for last."

Both laughed.

"Whatever," said Jasmine. "Where we going? To get a room?"

"You should have already known that," said Tarell.

Both laughed.

As Tarell drove by Lake Michigan on this hot summer night, Jasmine started to fantasize on riding Tarell. As they listen to Rapper Money bagg yo song play hard for the next, Jasmine felt so good. All good vibes. As they pulled into the Radisson Blu Aqua Hotel downtown. Jasmine started to feel nervous. She have not seen Tarell in 3 years and she's wondering how everything gonna be.

As they enter the Hotel, it was beautiful lighting, a huge pool and bar area. And oh my God the room had big windows, just everything jasmine liked. Tarell had already reserved the room for them. There was roses everywhere on the floor leading to the bed. A fruit tray with strawberries, that's her favorite, a bottle of Champagne.

Jasmine stood with her hand to her mouth. "Baby this is so sweet."

A bouquet of roses on the bed. He poured her a glass of Champagne. He handed it to her and they began to kiss.

Jasmine took a sip.

Tarell led her to the bathroom where he got her a Victoria Secret 2 piece set. Jasmine jumped in the shower and put on her new two piece set. Tarell was waiting on the bed for her. He played *Changes* by Her.

Jasmine was 5'4, brown skin with 22' hair, all black like he liked it. Tarell liked her slim, thick shape. Jasmine had a few tattoos, one of his name.

As Jasmine got into bed. Tarell reached for her and they began to kiss. They could feel the love they had for each other through their kisses. Tarell slowly started to take off her two piece set as they both got undressed.

Jasmine after seeing his 9' dick she couldn't help but give him head. Tarell eyes was closed.

Jasmine got on top and started to ride him for a while then he got on top and fold her legs like a pretzel. He went inside slow first then deeper and faster. The moans was very loud. They both came. Tarell laid back on the bed. And Jasmine laid on his chest and they began to talk about they wants.

"Look I know you sell drugs bae, but foreal you gotta find something else to do I can't go no more years of being without you," said Jasmine.

"I love you," said Jasmine.

"I love you too," said Tarell. "But this all I know and you don't have to worry I ain't going nowhere."

Jasmine took a deep breath she looked up at Tarell and he was sleep. So she closed her eyes and fell asleep too.

The next day Tarell and Jasmine got their things to check out. Tarell phone rung. "What's up?"

It was his Baby mama Shanice. His second Baby mama that can't leave him alone. Jasmine and her stayed into it. Jasmine listened as Tarell started to yell.

"Look bitch don't call my fucking phone no more with this shit. If ain't shit wrong with my son don't call me." Tarell hung up after.

"What's wrong bae?" asked Jasmine.

"Shanice ass talking bout somebody told her they seen us together yesterday."

"Really, wow," said Jasmine.

Tarell phone rung again but it was his Business phone. As they got into the truck, Jasmine text her girl's, "Where y'all at?"

Aneka text back first.

Aneka asked, "How was your night?"

"Bitch," said Jasmine.

lol both.

Chapter Four

"Where you at?" asked Markell, in a text to Jasmine.

"On my way home."

"Call me," Markell replied back.

"Good Morning, Dear." It was Brian

"Good Morning Baby," said his wife MYA.

They have been married for 8 years and have 3 children named Brian Jr, Destiny, and Nyah.

"So what time is Darnell party tonight?" asked Mya.

"Seven why?" asked Brian. "I thought you wasn't going Mya."

"Yeah I change my mind. My mother will watch the kids. So I'm gonna go."

"Okay baby," said Brian. Brian was nervous because he invited, Aneka to the party. He kissed his wife and 3 children goodbye. He left for work and immediately called Aneka.

"Hey baby," said Brian. "Bad news."

"What wrong?" asked Aneka.

"You can't come to the party with me tonight."

"What why?" asked Aneka. She was pissed!

"My wife changed her mind and decided to come out with me."

Aneka was silent for a moment then she asked, "What made her change her mind?"

"I don't know," said Brian. "But she's coming."

Aneka was pissed and refused to stay home. "Well look bae, I can still come. She don't know me. I haven't seen you in week since you left for your business trip."

"I know but I don't wanna risk us," said Brian.

"Look I'm gonna come. Me and a friend," said Aneka. "And when I get there me and you can sneak off somewhere."

Brian laughed. "Girl you dangerous. That's why I like you."

"That's why you what," said Aneka.

Brian laughed again. "I meant love bae."

"Ok I'll see you later," said Aneka. "I love you too."

Mya met Brian in high school. They had known each other forever. But she had not been happy in her marriage to Brian. She loved their children and their home. But Brian was not being the husband he used to. Mya was 5'7 skinny, light skin, long hair. She was an Attorney as well.

Mya phone rung. It was Erica one of her best friends.

"Hello," said Mya.

"Hey sweetie," said Erica. "How are you?"

"I'm good," replied Mya.

Erica was Adventurous. Mya wished she could be that way, but she was raised that a lady should be a lady. Never get loud in a public place, or use profanity. Erica was a free spirit. She was 29 and her boyfriend was 30. Erica was an owner of her on hair salon on the south side. Curtis was a Barber. He also owned his on shop on the south side of Chicago. Erica loved Curtis but she wasn't ready to have kids and Curtis was.

"So are you going to the party tonight?" asked Erica

"Yes," said Mya.

"Great," said Erica. "But I have something to tell you. I heard Brian was cheating on you with some bitch. Hood bitch named Aneka."

The phone went silent for a few seconds. Then Mya replied, "Are you serious?"

"Yes I am," said Erica.

"How do you know this?" asked MYA.

"Well I found out by my client which happens to be the Aneka girl mother."

"Tell me everything," Mya demanded.

"My client name is Mary. She came in for her noon appointment," said Erica. "And I asked her how was her day going so far. And she said lovely. She said her daughter Aneka usually brings her, which is true."

"And she replied with, she has a new boyfriend now name Brian Blake and he spoils her. And I asked her if he was Brian

Blake that works at WELLS & WELLS Law Firm. Yes honey said Ms. Mary, that's what everybody calls her. Ms. Mary said he got her daughter a new car, furnish her place, and she said he treats her daughter like a Queen. I didn't tell her I knew him. I just replied with 'Oh sounds like she has a good one.' Anyway I know who the bitch is Mya," said Erica. "And I know that you don't like confrontation, but you need to do something about this. How many times are you gonna let him keep doing this to you?"

Mya was crying on the other side of the phone.

"Look I love you girl and I got your back with everything," said Erica.

"You know he been cheating on me for years," said Mya. "And I'm so tired of it. But I'm still gonna go to the party anyway because Darnell is a great friend of ours."

Brian and Darnell and Mya all went to high school together, but Brian and Darnell were closer because they grew up together. And Darnell had always liked Mya. They kissed once in college, but Mya decided to date Brian. So Mya and Darnell just stayed friends.

Mya hung up from Erica. She looked in the mirror and began to cry. She just didn't understand why Brian kept cheating. Mya thought to herself, *I'm done with feeling this way.* She had a plan for Brian ass.

Mya got in the shower Afterwards, she put on a long red backless silk dress. It was a summer evening in June. Erica had did her hair a few days ago. Just a natural press. Mya put on her Chistian Louboutin heels open toe, then her phone rung again. It was Brian.

"Hello," said Mya.

"Hey Baby," said Brian. "Could you meet me at the party?"

"Sure," said Mya. "Is there a reason to why we can't go together?"

"I'm already downtown," said Brian. "So I can get dress at my office."

"Ok," said Mya.

"Are you ok Mya?" asked Brian. "You sound different."

"Yes I'm fine I'll meet you at the party."

"Okay," said Brian. "I love you."

Mya said, "I love you too."

Francesca was friends with Mya and Erica. She was more open mined than the other two. Francesca was a doctor. The youngest at her job. She delivered babies. She was single with no kids but wants it all, the family life.

Mya called Francesca.

"Hey luv are you ready yet?" asked Mya. "Well did you wanna ride with me? I'm gonna meet Brian at the party."

"Sure I'm gonna drive to you," said Francesca. "I'll be there in 15 mins."

Francesca only lived 15 mins away from Mya. Francesca pulled up in her 2020 Orange Porsche truck. She had on a Versace dress with the matching heels, she was brown skin, long hair, more thick than her friends. Francesca walked into Mya house.

"Hello," said Francesca. She had a bottle of 1942 Don Julio in her hand to take to Darnell because it was his birthday.

"Really Fran?" said Mya. "You got him something. Now I feel bad, because I didn't."

Both laughed.
"Well you know I can't go to a party without bringing something."

Both laughed.

"Well you know, just you being there is enough for him," said Fran to Mya.

"What?" said Mya.

"Girl, you know Darnell is sweet on you."

"No," said Mya. "That was a little crush a while ago."

"Yeah yeah," said Fran.

"How are things with you and Brian?" asked Fran.

Mya took a deep breath and said, "He's cheating again."

Tears was in her eyes but she refused to let them drop.

"I'm sorry Mya," said Fran. "How did you find out?"

"Erica told me," said Mya. "I don't know what to do. I'm so lost."

"I don't understand why men cheat on good women. You have his kids and you do whatever for him," said Fran.

"I know," said Mya. "I have a career, I take care of home, I cook dame."

"I can't believe Brian," said Fran. "After you all seen a therapist, I thought he change."

"No he got worse," said Mya.

"Well let's go have a good time tonight and leave our troubles behind," said Fran. "We will deal with this later."

"Okay," said Mya.

"Markell are you ready" asked Aneka.

"Yes bitch my kids with my mama. Pull up bitch," said Markell.

Aneka pulled up in a brand new Merced that Brian bought her.

Markell mouth dropped. "Bitch why you didn't tell me you got a new car?"

Aneka replied, "He got it for me a few weeks ago. I didn't bring it home because I wanted my name in the seats."

"Dame he really love your ass girl," said Markell.

A 2021 Red Mercedes Benz C Class Coupe.

"I can't wait to see my baby tonight," said Aneka. "Girl his wife will be there. But the bitch don't know about me."

Both laughed.

$$\cdot\!\!\!\!-\!\!\!\!\gg\!\!\times\!\!\ll\!\!\times\!\!\times\!\!\times\!\!\gg\!\!\times\!\!-\!\!\!\!\cdot$$

Chapter Five

Brian, pulled up to the four season's Hotel downtown Chicago. As he entered, Darnell was waiting for him there.

"Happy Birthday brother," said Brian.

"Thank you. Thank you," said Darnell.

As they entered, the party room everything was black and gold. Darnell was 6'1, Dark skin, nice muscles that drive most women crazy, a few tattoos and dreadlocks. He smelled so good he was wearing BURBERRY Fragrance. He had on a Armani suit with some red bottoms. A brand new Rolex watch. He was definitely a sight to see. There were a lot of people there at his birthday party. Darnell close family and friends.

Mya and Fran walked in, and Erica met them. She was already there with her boyfriend Curtis. Curtis was a barber shop owner. He was brown skin, nice low haircut, 5'10. He didn't care too much for her friends but he came for his girl Erica. He felt her friends were full of themselves.

As Erica walked over to her friends, she said, "Hello ladies."

Erica had on a Chanel dress with matching heels.

"Don't y'all look sexy," said Erica. "Let's get a drink."

As the three ladies hit the bar, Erica said to the bartender, "Can I have three glasses of Chardonnay?"

Brian walked over. "Hello my beautiful wife." And he kissed Mya on the cheek.

"Hello husband, how long have you been here?" asked Mya.

"Not long," said Brian. He could feel something was wrong with his wife but didn't pay it any mind.

"Where's Darnell?" said Mya. "I wanna tell him happy birthday."

"Let me run to the bathroom, then we can find him," said Brian.

"Ok," said Mya.

Brian didn't need to go to the bathroom. He went somewhere private to call Aneka.

Ring Ring.

"Hello," said Aneka.

"Hey baby, where are you?" said Brian.

"I'm almost there," said Aneka.

"Alright my wife has on a long red backless dress, when you see her stay away," said Brian. "Bae I don't wanna mess up my best friend birthday."

"I understand I'll see you soon," said Aneka.

"Alright love you baby," said Brian.

"I love you too," said Aneka.

When Brian came back into the party, he seen Mya and Darnell talking. Brian always knew that Darnell had a soft spot for Mya, but he never looked into it because Darnell was his best friend. Brian never knew that Mya and Darnell had kissed before back in college.

As he walked over to the both of them.

"You ok bae?" said Mya. "You was gone for a while."

"Yeah, yeah," said Brian. "Let's eat."

Darnell loved his R&B music so he had his DJ play all R&B music through the night. Darnell hit the dance floor and Chris brown song Heat was playing. Darnell used to dance in college. Everybody hit the dance floor.

Aneka and Markell walked in.

"Dame, this shit is lit," said Markell. "I swear I didn't think these bougie motherfuckers would be lit like this."

Markell was certified ghetto. She had long blue hair, she was dark skin. After having 4 kids, she kept her body tight. Men loved her. She stayed in the gym.

Aneka was so happy to be at the party. She was so anxious to see Brian.

"Let's get a drink," said Aneka to Markell.

At the bar was Curtis, Erica's boyfriend. Now Erica and Curtis relationship was on the rocks because Curtis wanted kids and Erica don't.

As the two ladies hit the bar, Markell asked the bartender for two shots. Curtis couldn't take his eyes off of her. Markell had on an all black body suit, see through with some Gucci sandals. Markell was a CNA.

"How you doing Queen?" asked Curtis.

"I'm good," said Markell.

"My name is Curtis Shaw. And yours?"

"I'm Markell White, but my friend's call me kell."

"Cool," said Curtis. "Can I call you kell?"

"Sure," said Markell.

"How do you know Darnell?" asked Curtis.

"I don't actually my friend know him," said Markell.

As Curtis and Markell continued to talk, Aneka seen Brian and he had seen her too. They eyes locked and Aneka smiled so big seeing him. She wanted to go over so bad but she also seen his wife.

Aneka had on a Chanel dress backless. Everybody there had on name brand clothes. Aneka loved that kind of crowd everybody had money and you could tell. She drank sex on the beach full of cherries. Darnell seen Aneka, he went over to say hello.

"Hey how are you," said Darnell.

"Happy birthday," said Aneka. "And I'm good and this party is amazing."

"Thank you," said Darnell. "I'm glad you could make it. You talk to Brian?"

"I know she's here," said Aneka.

Darnell just looked at her.

"Are you ok?" asked Darnell.

"Yeah, I'm good," said Aneka.

Chapter Six

Darnell could tell she was upset. So he offered her a drink.

"What you drinking?" asked Darnell.

"Ummm Patron would be nice," said Aneka.

So they walked to the VIP room and Darnell had the waitress bring Aneka her drink. Aneka texted Markell to come to the VIP room.

Right after Markell, Brian walked in him and his wife Mya. Mya knows Aneka name, but Aneka don't know that. Or Brian. Aneka smiled and left the VIP room. Fast. Markell was just walking to the VIP room, when Aneka grabbed her arm. "That's his wife."

"Are you foreal?" asked Markell.

Both laughed. Aneka tried to play it off like it was ok but she was very hurt seeing Brian with his wife.

"Did she say anything to you?" asked Markell.

"No the bitch don't know me," said Aneka.

And since Aneka name wasn't mentioned, Mya didn't know it was her.

"I seen you at the bar getting your mack on," said Aneka to Markell.

"He fine what he do?" asked Aneka.

"He own his own Barber shop," said Markell.

"Oh nice," said Aneka.

"Yeah," said Markell. "You know I'm about to take my boys there. Free haircuts shit."

Both laughed.

"He said he's gonna call me," said Markell. "Did you talk to Brian?"

"Not yet his bitch ass wife is on his heels," said Aneka.

Both laughed.

"I'm like bitch get the fuck off my man," said Aneka. "Let's stay for a while."

"Why Jasmine didn't come?" asked Markell.

"Too busy under Tarell ass," said Aneka. "Darnell is looking real good tho. But he is not my type, he's way too flashy for me."

"He cool but I would never fuck with a nigga like that," said Aneka.

Aneka text Brian. It read, "When am I gonna get a hug?"

Brian text back fast. "Meet me in the lobby," said Brian.

Aneka rush to the lobby and he was already there.

"Hey baby," said Brian, and hugged Aneka so tight she put her arms around his neck and kissed him.

"I missed you," said Aneka.

"I miss you too," said Brian.

"Will I see you later?" asked Aneka.

"Yes just be patient," said Brian.

As they gave each other one more kiss, Curtis was walking by. He was leaving the party. He couldn't believe Brian was cheating. He always admired Brian and Mya relationship, because he wanted to be married and have kids.

As Brian went back to the party, Erica walked by Aneka and said, "Don't I know you?"

Aneka stopped and stared at her, "And yeah you do my mother's hair."

"Right may I asked what are you doing here?" asked Erica.

"I'm here for a friend's party," said Aneka.

"Really?" said Erica.

Now Aneka was starting to get pissed.

"What's with all the questions?" asked Aneka.

"Did you attend Darnell party?"

"Yeah I did, and," said Aneka.

"How do you know him?" asked Erica.

"Is he your man or something?" asked Aneka.

"No," said Erica. "I just never seen you in our circle."

Aneka laughed and walked away. Markell was waiting for Aneka outside.

"Who was that?" asked Markell.

"Some bitch that does my mother hair. And her nosy ass was asking all these dame questions."

Erica went back inside to the party.

"Hey Fran," said Erica. "Where is Mya?"

"Mya left she wasn't feeling good," said Fran. "Is everything ok?"

"No," said Erica. "Brian had his bitch here."

"What," said Fran.

"YES," said Erica. "I'll tell you later."

As she went back out of the party, Curtis was waiting for her. As Erica got in the car with Curtis.

"Do you know that Brian is cheating on Mya?" said Erica.

"Yeah I seen him kissing some girl in the lobby," said Curtis.

"What," said Erica. "Curtis I can't believe that asshole. How could he bring a bitch to a place where his wife will be?"

"Because some men don't give no fuck," said Curtis.

"That's probably why Mya left the party," said Erica.

"Yeah that's crazy," said Curtis.

"And embarrassing," said Erica.

"But it's not our business," said Curtis.

"Wait what?" said Erica.

"Look we got our own problems," said Curtis.

"I know we need to work on things but that's my friend," said Erica.

"We need to focus on us if we really wanna make it Erica," said Curtis.

"I know you wanna get married and have kids Curtis, but I'm just not ready for all of that," said Erica. "We have our businesses and I just feel we should wait."

"Our businesses are doing well," said Curtis. Which is why we should start a family."

"I just don't wanna rush," said Erica.

"We been together for 5 years," said Curtis. "Really what are we waiting for?"

"Every time we talk about this it's an argument," said Erica.

As they drove home back to Hyde Park, you could feel the tension in the car.

As Aneka and Markell headed home, Aneka got a text from Brian.

"Hey baby meet at our spot," said Brian. Brian had a condo that Mya knew nothing about.

Aneka text back saying, "Ok bae. I'll be there as soon as I drop off Markell."

"Girl I can't wait to make love to my man tonight," said Aneka.

Both laughed.

"I wish I was getting some tonight," said Markell.

As Markell arrived at Markell appt, she got a text from Curtis.

"Hey love just making sure you got home safe," said Curtis.

Markell looked at her phone with a big smile.

"Bitch who got you smiling like that?" asked Aneka.

"Curtis," said Markell.

"The guy from the bar seems a bit thirsty," said Aneka.

Both laughed.

"Good night bitch be safe," said Markell.

Aneka pulled off and headed to Brian. As Aneka drove she began to think about how she hated seeing Brian with his wife. She wanted that spot of being his wife. As she got out of the new car Brian got her, she walked to the door and Brian was waiting on her with his boxers on, 6 pack showing, smelling good. Everything Aneka wanted to talk about just left her mind.

As she stepped inside, Brian grabbed her by her hips and kissed her once then looked in her eyes and kissed her again. They continue to hug and kiss and Brian picked her up and carried her to the bedroom.

He undressed her he began to kiss her everywhere. Aneka was in love with Brian.

After they finish making love, Aneka began to tell Brian how she felt about him. Then she asked, "When are you getting a divorce?"

"Bae really?" said Brian.

"Yes really Brian," said Aneka. "I can't keep going on like this Brian."

"Like what Neak?" said Brian.

"Sneaking around not being able to be seen together," said Aneka.

"Look let's talk about this in the morning," said Brian.

"Fine," said Neka.

But Aneka knew that wouldn't happen. Aneka fell asleep in Brian arms.

Brian phone was blowing up it was Mya. It was 2 am and he was not answering. So Mya called Darnell.

"What's up?" said Darnell.

"Hi, look I'm sorry for calling so late," said Mya. "Is Brian with you?"

"No," said Darnell.

Mya could still hear the music from Darnell party

"Wow the party still going on," said Mya.

Both laughed.

"We actually wrapping things up," said Darnell.

"Well Good night," said Mya.

As Darnell went back to his party, he notices that Fran was still there. Fran walked over to Darnell.

"You still here?" said Darnell.

Both laughed.

"Yeah, I'm a little tipsy tho," said Fran. "Your party was."

"Yeah, I'm surprised you are still here Ms. work a lot," said Darnell.

Chapter Seven

Francesca secretly liked Darnell. He was very attractive and charming.

"So do you have a ride home?" asked Darnell.

"No I came with Mya and she left me."

Both laughed.

"She didn't even tell me," said Francesca.

"Wow," said Darnell. "She just call me looking for Brian."

"Yeah I hear he's cheating again," said Francesca.

"Oh yeah?" said Darnell. "Let me take you home."

"Thank you," said Francesca. It's been a while since Francesca had been in a relationship and she hasn't had sex in so long, she was eyeing Darnell and was playing on giving him a ride later.

As they got to Francesca, home she invited him in. Francesca had a 3 bedroom and 3 bathroom Condominium.

Darnell agreed to come in.

Francesca poured some wine. Darnell liked Fran but only as a friend. After Francesca sip her wine she leaned in and kissed Darnell. He kissed her and gently pushed her back and said, "I like you but I'm not looking for anything."

"That's fine, I'm just wanting to have a good time tonight," said Fran.

So Fran began to walk him to her Master bedroom. She had him by his pants. She was so impressed with how he handled her. He took his time with her as he began kissing all over her. Fran couldn't help but catch feelings.

The next morning Darnell was up before her. Francesca slowly started to open her eyes.

"What's the rush?" asked Fran.

"I gotta handle some business this morning," said Darnell.

Darnell walked over to her in bed and gave her a kiss on the head. Fran was feeling so brand new. She knew that Darnell didn't want anything with her, but she thought maybe he could change his mind after last night. How could he not want something with her?

Once Darnell left, Fran called her friend.

"Hello," said Erica.

It was Fran to brag about her night with Darnell.

"What's going on girl," said Erica.

"I had a great night last night," said Fran. "Darnell came back to my place and oh my lord girl he hit every spot I never knew I had."

Both laughed.

"Wow," said Erica. "I didn't know you was feeling Darnell like that."

"Well I've always thought he was very handsome and last night I went for it."

"Fran I'm gonna call you later. It's Curtis calling," said Erica, as Erica clicked over.

"Hey bae," said Curtis. "I was wondering if I could take you to lunch?"

"Oh that's so sweet bae but I have a client at 12."

"How about dinner later?" asked Curtis. Darnell was getting fed up with Erica not having time for him.

"I'll let you know bae," said Erica.

After they hung up Curtis began to think of Markell, so he called her.

"Hello?" answered Markell.

"Good afternoon Queen," said Curtis. "How are you this is Curtis Shaw."

Now Markell was not into corny guy's but after having 4 kids, she was wanting to try something new. Like a nice guy but she would never tell her girl's Aneka or Jasmine. They wouldn't understand.

"Oh hello how are you?" asked Markell.

"I'm good I was hoping that you was available for lunch today," ask Curtis.

"Sure that would be nice," said Markell. "Where do you wanna meet."

"Meet," said Curtis. "I'm gonna pick you up just text me your address."

Markell laughed. "Ok." and did just that.

Not even 20 minutes later Curtis was pulling up. As Curtis pulled up in front of Markell apartment, she was already waiting on her porch. Markell got into his truck which was a Cadillac truck. Markell had on some white shorts and a blue top with her clear slides. Curtis had on white shorts and a white T.

Curtis loved how real Markell was. She was herself and didn't care what people thought of her unlike Erica. Curtis took Markell Downtown to a sports bar, they ordered food and drinks and ate outdoors.

"So tell me about yourself," said Curtis.

"Well I have 4 kids."

"4," said Curtis. "Wow that's beautiful."

Both laughed.

"Oh I thought that was a problem," said Markell.

"No I love kids I want a lot," said Curtis.

"I'm a CNA and thinking about going back to school to become a nurse," said Markell.

"Nice my mother was a nurse," said Curtis. "She also had 4 kids so I get it."

"So tell me a little more about you," said Markell.

"Are you seeing anybody?" asked Markell.

"Yes," said Curtis. "But we are not seeing eye to eye anymore. I want marriage and kids and she don't."

"Oh," said Markell.

After lunch was over Curtis took Markell home

"We have to do this again," said Curtis.

"Yes," said Markell. "And the next lunch will be on me."

As Markell walked into her apartment her phone rung it was Jasmine. She was walking to Markell apartment and seen her get out of this Red Cadillac truck.

"Bitch who just drop you off?" said Jasmine. "Matter fact come open the door."

Markell opened her door.

"I met him downtown." said Markell. "At the party me and Aneka went to."

"Oh yeah how was the party?" asked Jasmine.

"Lit for a bunch of bougie motherfuckers."
Both laughed.

"Speaking of Aneka here she come."

She pulled up playing Jasmine Sullivan song On It.

"Yesss bitch that's my song," said Markell.

Aneka got out of her car and let the music play as she went and set on Markell porch.

"What you Hoes up to?" said Aneka.

"Shit," said Markell.

"I just got back from lunch with my new Li friend Curtis."

"What?" said Aneka. "Ok bitch."

"Dame, he really like you or thirsty for some ass from you," said Aneka. Both laughed.

"Girl stop," said Markell. "He different."

"Why you say that?" asked Aneka.

"Well he don't have any kids and he wants to get married," said Markell. "Like these niggas ain't on that."

"True," said Aneka.

"But he do have a girl," said Markell. "And she don't want kids or marriage."

"His girl."

"Red flag bitch," said Jasmine. "If he has a girl why the fuck is he with you? I knew he sounded too good to be true. Lunch calling you Queen and shit them fuckboy words period."

"I know," said Markell. "But he said him and the bitch are on the rocks."

Both laughed.

"Dame," said Markell.

Brian had just got home wondering what he was gonna tell Mya he had been. As he stepped inside, he noticed that Mya and the kids was gone. He called her name but no answer, then he seen a note on the table that read:

"I want a divorce since you can't keep your dick in your pants. I'm done. Me and the kids are fine. I will be back for the rest of our things have a nice life."

Brian couldn't believe it. He was in shock. He never thought Mya would leave him. He thought she was too weak to leave. So Brian called his best friend.

"What's up?" said Darnell.

"Mya left me I can't believe this," said
Brian. "She took my kids, she left a note
saying she wants a divorce."

Brian was losing his mind.

"Calm down," said Darnell. "I thought you
wanted out?"

"I thought I did," said Brian. "But now
that she left, I know I don't want this. I
don't believe this shit."

"Did you go home last night?" asked
Darnell.

"No why?" asked Brian.

"Well Mya called me looking for you," said
Darnell.

"Dame I was with Neka."

"Let me hit you back." It was Darnell
other line.

"Hello?" said Darnell.

It was Fran. "Heyy I was wondering if you
wanted to do dinner later?"

"Yeah that would be cool," said Darnell.

"Ok like 7. Let's I'll call you," said Fran.

Mya called Erica. "Where are you? I left
Brian."

"Really look I know you and Brian have
been together for a while but I'm glad y'all is
over," said Erica. "Brian had the bitch at
the party."

"What?" said Mya. "Are you serious?"

"Yes," said Erica. "I tried to tell you but
you had already left."

Mya began to scream and cuss. Erica never heard her friend talk like that she was worried.

"I can't believe he would do this shit," said Mya.

"I know," said Erica.

"Who is she how did she look?" asked Mya.

"She had on Chanel," said Erica.

"Really Erica?" said Mya. "A lot of women was wearing Chanel."

"I told her ass a few words," said Erica.

"Oh my God how could Brian Be so disrespectful," said Mya.

Mya was crying so hard

"Where are you staying?" asked Erica.

"My mother's me and the kids."

"I'm coming over have you heard from Fran today?" asked Erica.

"No," said Mya.

"I'm gonna call her," said Erica.

And she did.

"Hello?" answered Fran.

It was Erica

"Hey Fran, look Mya needs us tonight. She left Brian and is really broken about it."

"I can't," said Fran. "I have plans tonight."

"More important than our best friend?" said Erica.

"Look we been here before with Mya and Brian," said Fran. "Mya is only gonna take him right back."

"It doesn't matter. She is our girl and she needs us tonight."

"Sorry I can't," said Fran, and she hung up

Erica was so pissed at Fran for not coming through.

Brian called and texted Mya phone about 10 times each. Mya still didn't respond.

"I know I fucked up again but I can't lose you and the kids," said Brian. "I love you so much I'll die without you please come home we can work this out."

Brian was begging through texts. Mya read them all but didn't respond. She wasn't gonna fall for his shit this time'

Mya called Darnell but no answer. She left a voice message that said, "Hey it's Mya, call me."

Aneka called Brian.

"Hello?" said Brian.

"Hey baby," said Aneka. "How are you?"

"I'm not so good Neka look we need to break things off," said Brian.

"Why?" asked Aneka. "What's going on Brian?"

"Me and my wife are going through somethings."

"Oh now you calling her your wife," said Aneka.

"She's always been my wife Aneka," said Brian. "Aneka I'm not gonna argue with you. It's over, we are done."

"Are you serious?" said Aneka.

Brian hung up

Aneka couldn't believe it. After everything, it was over. She didn't cry. She was too piss to do so.

Jasmine was sitting next to her. "What's wrong Neka."

But Aneka didn't say a word.

Chapter Eight

As nighttime came, Erica canceled dinner with Curtis. Her friendship was more important than her boyfriend she felt.

Francesca got ready for her date with Darnell. Do me baby was playing by prince as she waited for Darnell. 30 minutes went by and she had already sent countless text messages. She even called. Darnell never responded.

Fran was so confused because they spent a night together and he accept her dinner date. She couldn't call her girls because she had stood them up for Darnell.

Curtis was at his breaking point. He called Markell and asked her to dinner and he included her children.

"I know we just met," said Curtis. "But I would love to take you and your kids to dinner tonight."

Markell felt so special. She had 4 kids and never did any man she ever went on a date with even ask how her kids was doing.

"That's really sweet of you Curtis but my kids are at a birthday party tonight."

"Ok," said Curtis. "Next time."

Then both laughed.

"So are you available?" asked Curtis.

"Of course," said Markell.

Markell was impressed with Curtis' consistency. She's use to hood niggas but this was something different.

"So can I pick the spot tonight?" said Markell.

"Yeah anywhere just name the place."

"Harold's Chicken."

Now if you from the Chi, everybody eat Harold's Chicken.

"Ok cool that's my spot," said Curtis.

Both laughed.

"And it's on me," said Markell.

Both laughed.

"Well I'm on my way," said Curtis.

Markell was dressed and couldn't wait to see him. She was definitely feeling him. Curtis pulled up and Markell jumped right in. They headed to Harold's Chicken.

"So how was your day?" asked Markell.

"It was cool. I'm not gonna lie to you. I really like you, and me and my girlfriend, we just not for each other."

"Wow straight to the point," said Markell.

Both laughed.

"Well I like you too. If you really wanna try something with me, then once you leave her, we can move forward," said Markell.

"Ok," said Curtis just like that.

As they pulled in front of Harold's Chicken, Markell had called it in so she got out and got the food. They ate in the car and talked about everything.

Curtis took Markell home. Markell kissed Curtis. She felt like a teenager again.

Curtis went home and told Erica it was over.

"Are you serious?" asked Erica.

"Yes we just not on the same shit no more Erica."

"You really leaving me? Who is the bitch Curtis?" asked Erica.

Curtis just walked out. He didn't wanna tell her that he did meet someone.

Erica was lost for words. She didn't like showing her pain to people. She stayed at home without even going to see Mya.

Jasmine wasn't feeling well. She called Tarell.

"Whattup?" said Tarell.

"Bae I don't feel well," said Jasmine. "Could you take me to the store?"

"Yeah give me a minute," said Tarell.

"Ok," said Jasmine.

Jasmine called Aneka.

"Heyy boo," said Aneka

"I think I'm pregnant," said Jasmine.

"What," said Aneka.

"Yes I been so sick for 3 weeks," said Jasmine. "Tarell on his way to take me to the store. I'm gonna get a pregnancy test."

"Oh he know?" asked Aneka.

"Not yet," said Jasmine. "I really love him, Neak."

Aneka had a flash back of her and Brian and what she thought they would have. Tarell wasn't far and he had one of his guy's with him and he began to tell him how he felt about Jasmine.

"I gotta take Jasmine to the store real quick," said Tarell to his friend J R.

"That's cool," said J R.

"Man I love Jasmine but after doing my time I don't think I wanna really be with her."

"Why you say that?" asked J R.

"Cause man Jasmine don't do shit man," said Tarell. "She just out here hustling like a nigga. She wear all this name brand shit. I know niggas buying it for her, aside of the shit her and her hoe ass friends be stealing."

"I want a woman that's doing something for herself. Not no bum ass bitch," said Tarell.

J R laugh. "Dame bro well leave her ass then."

Tarell pulled up to Jasmine mom house and Jasmine came out slow.

"Hurry up man," said Tarell. "I got shit to do."

"What's wrong with you?" asked Jasmine.

Tarell just pulled off heading to the store. Tarell had his music blasting. Tarell was smoking, him and J R.

As they got to the store Jasmine got out and she got a few snacks and the pregnancy test.

When she went back to the car, Tarell pulled off so fast.

"Dame what's your rush?" asked Jasmine.

"I told you I had something to do." Tarell didn't have anything to do. He was just going over his Baby mama house Shanice. Francesca was heading to the East side to see her mother Rachel. Her mother loved the hood. That's why she still lived there even tho she didn't have to. Her daughter was a doctor.

"Hello mother," said Fran.

"Heyyy baby I have not seen you in a while."

Fran only comes to see her mother every two months. Well she's a doctor and her mother did live in the hood.

"What brings you by?" asked Rachel.

"Well I missed your crazy butt," said Fran. "Do you need anything mom?"

"No I'm good. You don't see me much but I get them deposit tho."

Both laughed.

Fran always made sure her mother was taking care of and her two sisters and brothers. Fran was the oldest of her siblings

A guy pulled up and it was her old childhood friend Tarell. They mothers lived next door to each other since they were kids.

"Well hello there," said Fran.

"Wow," said Tarell. "I haven't seen you in so long."

He hugged Fran

Fran liked Tarell but they were so different. Tarell liked Fran but ended up going to jail before he could tell her.

"What brings you to the hood?" asked Tarell.

"Oh my really to see my mother," said Fran.

"We should go out," said Tarell.

"Ok I'm gonna stay at my mom place for the night. So if you wanna get breakfast tomorrow morning that's fine," said Fran.

Tarell took Fran number and went into his mom house. Fran was still hurt by Darnell standing her up but now that she seen Tarell, her mind was on Tarell.

"I seen you out there hugging Tarell," said Rachel.

"Yes I haven't seen him for a while," said Fran.

"I always thought y'all looked good together," said Rachel.

"Ma," said Fran.

"He is different from when we were kids. He stay in jail too much for me."

"Girl get off the high horse. You not seeing nobody and it's time for you to settle down."

"Yeah a doctor with a thug," said Fran.

Both laughed.

"I'm not saying necessarily settle down with Tarell, but it's time for you to date again."

Fran knew that Tarell would not be her husband but she was still gonna go out with him anyway. After all he was an old friend. Fran felt bad about standing up Mya for a man, so she called her.

"Hello?" said Mya.

"Hi," said Fran. "How are you?"

"I'm good," said Mya. "Brian is still calling and begging. I don't know if I should answer or what."

"Follow your heart Mya," said Fran. "You two love each other and you have kids. Are you sure you wanna give up 10 years of marriage?"

"No, I'm not sure," said Mya.

Mya began to think hard about what should she do. Nobody knew how hurt and tired she was with Brian. She was gonna take him back but she was going back a different person.

Chapter Nine

Jasmine was so nervous about finding out if she was having Tarell baby. Even tho it's what she wanted, she knew Tarell might not be so happy.

Aneka phone rung, it was Jasmine

It was positive. She was pregnant.

"Congrats," said Aneka. "How do you feel?"

"I'm happy but scared to tell him," said Jasmine.

"Just do it. What could he do," said Aneka.

"You right this could bring us closer," said Jasmine. "Maybe I'll tell him over the weekend."

"That would be good omg my bitch preggo," said Aneka.

Aneka was playing it cool, not showing how hurt she was over Brian leaving her.

The next day Aneka ran into Brian at his favorite bar downtown.

"Hi," said Aneka. "Why haven't I heard from you."

I been going threw a lot Neka," said Brian. "Work, my wife not letting me see my kids it's hard."

"I understand Brian," said Aneka. "But what about us?"

She was so in love with Brian.

"You said you was leaving her," said Aneka.

"Look Anek. I gotta go, I can't do this right now," said Brian. "I'll call you when I figure things out."

Aneka left the bar and walked into Darnell.

"Hey Darnell."

He was wrapped arm and arm with girl. "What's up Aneka?"

"How you been?" Aneka asked.

"Good and you," said Darnell.

"Look can I call later?" asked Aneka.

"Yeah," said Darnell. He gave her his number and walked off.

Mya called Darnell

"Hey how are you?" asked Mya.

"I'm good," said Darnell. "I should be asking you that."

"Look I know you had sex with Francesca," said Mya. "And I know it's not my business but why? I mean I just didn't know you liked her."

"I mean I like her but not to make my woman she not my type," said Darnell.

"Oh well she likes you and you should call her. Just say something," said Mya.

Both laughed.

"I will," said Darnell.

After she hung up from Darnell, Brian called.

"Bae look I really miss you and want you to come home," said Brian. "Baby please don't do this. Can I take you to dinner?"

Brian really wanted to do right this time.

"Fine," said Mya.

"I'll pick you up at 7," said Brian.

Curtis Called Markell. When Markell picked up, Curtis said, "I left my girl."

"Oh really in shock," said Markell. "Now what?"

Curtis said, "I'm on my way."

Markell was happy she finally found someone who cared.

Chapter Ten

Brian arrived at Mya parent's house. Brian was about to walk inside, when he seen his wife come outside.

"Hello," said Mya.

Brian hugged Mya. Mya was still upset but she did miss him too. As they headed to a local restaurants. The ride was tense. Mya was quiet but decided to break the ice.

"How was work?" asked Mya.

"It was a good day I got some new clients my firm is doing well."

"That's Great," said Mya.

When Brian pulled into a Cafe he parked and said, "We been together for 10 years and it hasn't been perfect but what is?"

Brian promised himself that if his wife took him back, he would do right.

"I Love You and I'm sorry."

Mya kissed her husband and took him back he had cheated before but she never left

He actually felt what it would be like without her, he couldn't stand it. They skipped dinner and went and got the kids from her parents' house. Then went home and made love like it was the first time.

Mya never asked him about his side showing up at Darnell party. She decided to keep it to herself. Brian thought everything was back together again. But he didn't know that he hurt her in a different way this time. She took him back, he was gonna pay for all the lies, cheating, and disrespect.

Curtis pulled up to Markell place. He seen a guy leaving. It was Markell baby dad. Curtis knew who he was because Markell had told him that he's the only one of her kids dad that show up.

Markell seen Curtis and she let him come inside

"So it's really over?" asked Markell.

"Yes," said Curtis, he kissed Markell.

Aneka called Darnell.

"Hello?" said Darnell.

"Hey Darnell, it's Aneka. Look I know that you was against me and Brian being together because he was married."

"It's more than that he's wife is a longtime friend of mine. Me and Brian are childhood friends but she's special to me," said Darnell.

"Oh," said Aneka. "You sound like you love her."

Aneka laughed, but Darnell didn't say a word.

"Well umm," said Aneka. "Me and Brian are over. I really love Brian and he told me he was leaving her."

"Yeah he not ever leaving his wife," said Darnell.

Aneka was lost for words. She's usually in control but she was so lost with this. She believed Brian was her soulmate.

"Look Aneka I gotta go," said Darnell.

Jasmine was getting ready to tell Tarell about the baby news. She decided to tell him now. As she went to dial his number, he was calling.

"What's up," said Tarell.

"Hey bae I was about to call you," said Jasmine. And before you knew it Jasmine just spit it out.

"Look I'm pregnant," said Jasmine. "Are you mad?"

"No but I didn't want no more kids, like I got 3 already," said Tarell.

"I know but I thought we was moving forward," said Jasmine.

"I just came home from prison and I'm trying to get shit together," said Tarell.

"Well what you want me to do?" said Jasmine.

"Shit it's up to you," said Tarell.

Jasmine hung up the phone. She was hurt and mad that Tarell wasn't happy about they baby. She laid on her Queen size bed and thought to herself what would she do if Tarell out of their relationship. What would she do? She had no job and lived with her mother and sisters. All of her sisters had kids. Her mother house was already packed now, here she come with a child.

The next day Fran met with Tarell. They went to a spot in the area for breakfast.

"Can I start you two with some drinks?" said the waitress.

"Yes I'll have a ice water," said Fran.

"I'll take a ice tea," said Tarell. "So it's been a long time."

"Yes it has," said Fran. "How many kids you have now?"

Both laughed.

"Three and one on the way."

"Wow well, I'm not surprised."

"What you mean?" asked Tarell.

"Well you always had a lot of women."

Both laughed. Fran couldn't help to stare at how Tarell had such a great smile. He smell so good after they ate. They hugged. Tarell kissed Fran on the cheek.

"It was good seeing you," said Fran. "Come see me sometime."

"I will," said Tarell.

Fran headed home and called Mya.

"Hello," said Mya.

"Hey how are you?"

"I'm better," said Mya. "Me and Brian are patching things up."

"Well good for y'all," said Fran.

"Look I'm gonna have to call you later," said Mya.

As Brian was getting ready for work. He heard Mya and the kids in the kitchen eating breakfast that made Brian smile. He was so glad he had his family back.

"Good morning bae," said Brian. "Any plans for today?"

"No," said Mya.

"Well let's go shopping and enjoy the day me you and the kids," said Brian.

"You hate shopping," said Mya.

"Look I owe my family," said Brian. "I'm calling in today and I'm spending time with my family."

Brian was happy to be home but he noticed a change in his wife. She been getting phone calls and taking them in the other room. He wondered why, but didn't ask because how could he after all his shit.

As they got the kids ready to get in the truck, Aneka was calling. Brian sent her to voicemail.

"Who was that?" asked Mya.

"Nobody," said Brian. Then a text came through.

Mya just shook her head after looking at Brian.

"Put on your seat belts, kids," said Mya.

Aneka text read: "It's killing me not to be able to see you smell you and hear your voice. I really love and miss you baby call me," said Aneka text.

"What's going on?" asked Aneka mother.

"You haven't left the house in two days. Is it about Brian?" asked Aneka mother.

"Yeah ma, he left me," said Aneka.

"Really you guys seem so happy," said Aneka's mother Mary.

"Yes but he left me to work things out with his wife. He said he was leaving her but..."

And Aneka's mother just cut her off. Her mother understood her pain but couldn't talk about it because it reminded her of Anek's dad who was married and told her the same thing. He was leaving his wife. He never did, but he left Aneka mother pregnant with her. She never healed from that.

"You will find better," said Aneka mother.

Chapter Eleven

The next day Brian left for work. And Mya took the kids to school. After dropping the kids at school Mya stopped at the store to get some wine, then she headed to a hotel. Waiting for her was Darnell.

As she pulled up in her silver Mercedes, Darnell got out of his Black Mercedes and opened her door.

"Hey baby," said Darnell.

After Darnell party, Mya called him looking for Brian. After Darnell left Fran house, the business he told Fran he had to take care of, was Mya.

She texted him in pain, he went to her fast. He never called Fran back because he hooked up with Mya that day he told Fran he would go to dinner with her. After sleeping with Mya, he told her, he was in love with her.

Mya told him she was taking Brian back. Darnell understood but really wanted to be with her but he wouldn't get in the way of what she wanted. And the next day, Aneka had bumped into Darnell with someone else who he cared nothing about.

Darnell was in love with Mya and she was in love with him too. However she wasn't gonna end her marriage just yet. She still had other plans for Brian.

As they entered the hotel where they had been meeting each other for a few weeks, Darnell kissed her once they entered the room.

"How are the kids?" asked Darnell.

"They are good bae."

"So what do I owe the pleasure of seeing you this morning?" asked Darnell.

"I'm pregnant," said Mya.

"Are you sure?" asked Darnell. Darnell was happy and confused this would be his first child but dame with his friend wife.

"What are we gonna do?" asked Darnell.

"I'm keeping our baby," said Mya.

"Are you sure it's mine?" asked Darnell.

"Yes, I only use condoms with Brian," said Mya.

Mya phone rung it was Brian but she didn't answer.

Brian set back in his chair at work, he could feel something was wrong but couldn't put his finger on it.

Mya and Darnell decided to keep their baby and their secret of them messing around between them. Mya left the hotel and headed home. She knew she had to tell Brian about the baby because you can't hide a baby.

Brian was so happy to hear about his wife being pregnant with so he thought their 4th child.

"Baby I knew something was going on with you," said Brian. He kissed Mya.

Brian called everybody and told them their good news.

Mya was feeling in control now. Brian was getting to play the fool and she was enjoying it.

After months went by Mya had a boy. She named him Dontae. Brian didn't care for the name but he wasn't complaining. He was happy that him and Mya was back together.

Markell and Curtis moved in a new place together and got married. She is having Curtis first child. It's a girl.

Erica, Curtis ex, heard about it and pretended to be happy but she was upset at herself that she didn't pay more attention to her relationship.

Jasmine had a boy with Tarell and she named their son. Jarell they are still together.

Aneka is still single and she has not got over Brian but you couldn't tell, she still go out and acted as if she never knew him even tho it kills her inside how he left.

Fran is dating a doctor and never understood why Darnell never called her back. She still sends hello texts every now again.

Darnell and Mya are still seeing each other.

And Brian still don't know that baby Dontae isn't his!

About the Author

Latisha Miller was born in Evergreen Park, Illinois. She was raised in Chicago, the Roseland area. She has lived in Gary IN. Latisha moved to Madison, WI in 2007. When Miller was eighteen, she left and returned home to live with her parents Raul and Cynthia in Valparaiso, just after giving birth to her first child, a daughter, Haseena. Latisha moved back to Madison WI in July 2009, and it was a great move at the time. She found her first apartment, her first car, and it was great. Miller is hoping to move back home to the "Chi" one day, as Chicago will always have her heart. .Latisha has lived in Madison, WI for 14 years. She is ready to go back to the chi and continue her journey of writing new books. She is now a mother of two to Haseena and Camren.

www.ingramcontent.com/pod-product-compliance
Lightning Source LLC
Chambersburg PA
CBHW051823130726

47987CB00003B/1382